☆ molly&mimi ☆

Tantrums and Tiaras

For soggy moggies the world over,
you have my sympathies – S.H.

STRIPES PUBLISHING
An imprint of Magi Publications
1 The Coda Centre, 189 Munster Road,
London SW6 6AW

A paperback original
First published in Great Britain in 2008

Text and illustrations copyright © Sarah Horne, 2008

ISBN: 978-1-84715-045-5

Printed and bound in Germany.

10 9 8 7 6 5 4 3 2 1

Tantrums and Tiaras

Sarah Horne

stripes

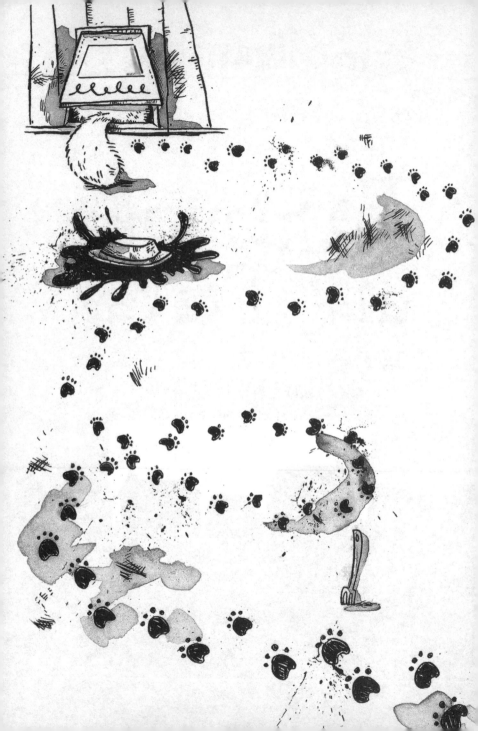

Life is full of surprises,
and these can come in all shapes and sizes.

 surprises,

small surprises,

surprises, **bad**
surprises,

and the rarest of all ...

impossible-to-believe
surprises.

And just who would
have believed in a talking cat...?

Chapter One

Palace Von Volavon

"Hill, tree ... another tree ... sheep, cows. Boring!" sniffed Molly Potsome as she gazed out of the car window. She wriggled uncomfortably in her seat, squished between a bookshelf and a crusty old leather trunk. "Are we nearly there yet?" she moaned.

"Almost," said Dad. "Look, there's a sign for Fuffleton."

"Cool," said Molly. Although the countryside was boring, she couldn't wait to see her new house and start exploring.

The car heaved itself up a steep country lane and shuddered to a halt in front of a pretty stone cottage. The windows were painted jade green and a curtain of pretty yellow roses hung around the door.

☆ molly&mimi ☆

Everyone piled out of the car.

"Here we are!" cried Mum excitedly.

"Our lovely new home!" said Dad.

"What do you think, Molly?"

But Molly didn't answer.

Something else had caught her eye...

"WOW!"

Molly gasped, pointing to the house next door.

It was the most fantastic house she had ever seen. It glistened with jewels from top to toe and flags fluttered from the turrets. The stained-glass windows glinted in the sunlight. And on top of the solid gold gates, in the swirliest of writing, were the words: Palace Von Volavon.

"A palace!" exclaimed Molly. "Who do you think lives there?

It must be a princess,

or maybe even a queen."

"Perhaps," said Mum, smiling. "It's certainly different."

Molly stood spellbound as Mum and Dad staggered past, struggling with boxes, trunks and plant pots.

"Come on, Molly, aren't you going to help?" puffed Dad. "The sooner we get unpacked, the sooner you can explore."

"OK, coming," she sighed. She was just about to go, when she felt somebody standing behind her. She turned round and came face to face with a very wrinkly, very crinkly old man.

"**Beware, Miss, beware!**" he said in a shaky voice.

"Beware of what?" asked Molly.

"The Fiend of Fuffleton, of course!
There's a little **Beastie** in there,"
said the old man, leaning on his walking
stick and pointing with a crooked,
knobbly finger at the palace. "A nasty
little creature, with very sharp teeth and
claws. So just you

beware!"

Then he turned
and hobbled away.
"Wow!" said
Molly, beaming
with excitement.
"A Beastie *and*
a palace!
How cool!"

Chapter Two

New Neighbours

"Achoooo." Molly sneezed as she rummaged through the boxes in her bedroom. She reached into the nearest one and lifted out a dusty pile of books.

Her new room was up in the attic and had a lovely sloping ceiling and pretty light-blue walls. But the best thing about it was that she could see the palace from the window.

Molly stared up at the turrets. Could there be a princess locked inside...? Or was that where the Beastie lived?

Mum had promised that she'd take Molly to meet the neighbours if they finished unpacking before teatime.

Molly gazed around her room – what a mess! She'd never finish unpacking by then. Keeping an eye out for Mum, she emptied out the boxes on to the floor and shovelled everything under her bed. It didn't all fit, so she swept the last few things under the rug. Her mum would never know!

Molly rushed downstairs. "Mum, I've finished!" she called. "Can we go next door to the palace?"

Mum looked at Molly's hopeful face. "Why not," she said, handing Dad her duster. "I could do with a break."

Molly stood on the Von Volavons' doorstep, hopping with excitement, as she waited for Mum to catch up. The door had a huge brass knocker in the shape of a cat's head. She reached up and knocked once … twice … three times, and was just about to knock again when Mum grabbed her hand.

"I'm sure they heard you, Molly."

There was a click of high-heels, and a moment later, the door opened just a crack.

A woman's head poked out. She looked Molly and her mum up and down.

"Yes?" she snapped, opening the door a little wider. "Are you from the school? Are you the girl who's accused my Saffron of pulling her hair?"

Molly stared. The woman was huge and round, dressed from head to toe in bright pink – pink high-heel shoes and a pink polka-dot dress – and with her fluffy blonde hair, she reminded Molly of a giant stick of candyfloss. Her fingers dripped with jewels and her ears sparkled with the biggest diamonds Molly had ever seen.

Mum laughed nervously. "Oh no, we're not from the school, we're your new neighbours at number 24. I'm Pamela Potsome and this is Molly. We thought we'd just pop by and say hello."

Molly smiled at the lady and said the first thing that came into her head. "We went to the funfair last week, and I had some candyfloss just like your hair."

There was a long, awkward pause.

From inside, Molly could hear children's voices.

"I can't believe you're scared of a cat," a girl's voice taunted. "Scaredy-cat, scaredy-cat!"

"Am not," a boy replied.

"So why won't you feed Mimi, then? It's your turn, Dylan," the girl sneered.

"Is not. I fed her yesterday," the boy whinged.

"Did not!"

"Did, did, did…"

"Not, not, not times infinity!"

There was silence, and then an ear-splitting howl.

"Mum, he hit me," whimpered the girl.

The candyfloss lady swivelled her head. "Shut your noise, Saffron! Do you want our new neighbours to hear you and your brother whinging and whining?" She turned back to her visitors and plastered a smile on her face.

"I'm Mrs Von Volavon. Very nice to meet you."

"You, too," said Mum. She smiled
weakly. "Perhaps you'd like to pop round
and see us sometime. And do bring the
children – you'd love to meet them,
wouldn't you, Molly?"

Molly was about to reply, but Mrs
Von Volavon got in first. "Yes-that'd-be-
lovely-see-you-then-bye!"

The next moment the door slammed
shut, and Molly and her mum were left
standing on the doorstep.

"Goodness," said Mum. "I don't think
she's a queen or a princess!"

She took Molly by the hand and
steered her down the path, round a very
grand fountain. It had a large, gleaming
bronze fish at its centre, which every
now and then fired water from its
mouth. Molly had never seen anything
quite like it.

As they closed the gates, Molly stole one last peek at the palace. Just at that moment something large, white and ridiculously fluffy flashed across one of the stained-glass windows.

Strange, thought Molly.

Chapter Three

Family Von Volavon

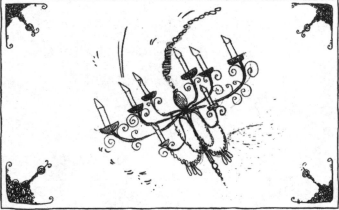

Mrs Von Volavon stood in the hallway, fuming. Up above her the chandelier swung dangerously, as footsteps thundered across the landing.

"Where are you, you little horrors? Come down here this instant!" she boomed. "I'm going to count to five. ONE – TWO – THREE – FOUR – FI—"

A door flew open with a bang, and a
pinker-than-pink girl trotted down
the stairs.

"Muuum," she
whined in a
small, pathetic
voice.

"I WANT
A PONY!"

"Quiet, Saffron," said her mother sharply. "I've already said you're not having a pony until your birthday."

Saffron stared, narrowing her eyes. "You mean I have to wait TWO WEEKS? That's so NOT fair! I'm going to ask Dad." She turned and stomped over to her dad's study, and flung open the door. "Daaaaaddy!" she wailed.

Mr Von Volavon was almost hidden behind a large pile of papers. He was a small man with an ink-smudged face, and he spent most of his time plotting money-making schemes and keeping as far away from his family as possible.

"Saffron, darling," he said, without looking up. "Is anything the matter?"

"Yes," she pouted. "Mum says I can't have a pony until my birthday."

Mr Von Volavon sighed and did what

he always did when confronted by one of his children – he pretended not to hear.

The next minute, a boy appeared on the landing and bounded down the stairs.

"Muuuuuum – I've got my finger stuck!" he cried.

"Well you shouldn't have put it up there in the first place," said Mrs Von Volavon.

"But MUM!" he snivelled, yanking her arm with his free hand.

"It hurts."

Saffron tugged at her mum's other arm. "Daddy says I can have a pony NOW!"

At that, Mrs Von Volavon turned a violent shade of purple. "Right, that's it! I've had enough. We're going on holiday. Clive!" she shouted.

"Yes, dear?" replied Mr Von Volavon, from the other room.

"Remember that place we went to, where we stayed on one island and the children were on another? Book the tickets. I want to leave as soon as possible."

"Of course, dear, right away!"

An air of calm fell on the Von Volavon household. All was well.

For about five seconds, that is.

Mrs Von Volavon frowned. "What about Mimi?" she said. "Who's going to look after that dreadful powder-puff, pain-in-the-neck cat?"

Chapter Four

An Unexpected Visitor

"So how was the palace?" asked Dad. "Did you get to meet the princess?"

"Not exactly!" said Molly, as she crammed her mouth full of fish and chips. "And we only got to peek inside."

"I think we visited at a bad time," said Mum, "but I told Mrs Von Volavon to pop over with the children any time."

"There's a boy and a girl, but I only

heard them. They were shouting at each other," said Molly, matter of factly, shovelling peas with her fork. "And Mrs Von Volavon slammed the door on us. But hopefully next time we'll get to go inside the palace."

"Hmmm, yes," said Mum, "we didn't get off to the best of starts, but I'm sure they're lovely people really."

She gave Dad a look, and mouthed the word **RUDE**.

Just then, there was a sharp knock at the door. "Visitors! At this time?" sighed Dad.

"I'll get it," said Molly, jumping down from the table. She hurried into the hall and heaved the door open.

Mrs Von Volavon filled the porch.

"Oh, hello," said Molly politely. "We were just talking about you. Would you like to come in?"

Mum stared in surprise, as Molly led Mrs Von Volavon through to the kitchen. "Oh, Mrs Von Volavon, how unexpected."

She collected up the half-finished plates, leaving Dad staring longingly at his disappearing chips. "This is my husband, Peter. Do take a seat."

Mrs Von Volavon perched her huge bottom on a kitchen stool, which wobbled dangerously.

"It's really Molly I've come to see," she said, patting Molly on the head.

How would you like to take care of my daaarling cat, Mimi, while we're away on holiday? She's a gorgeous pure-bred Persian, and she'll really be no trouble at all. She just needs feeding and a little entertaining.

Molly could hardly believe her luck. *This is my chance to see inside the palace*, she thought. *Cat-sitting – how difficult can that be? All I've got to do is feed Mimi and play with her.*

"Oh yes please!" she said out loud. "I love cats!"

Mum gave Molly a puzzled look. "Are you sure, Molly? Only, you've never had a pet before."

"Oh yes, positive. What do I have to do?"

"Don't worry about that now," said Mrs Von Volavon, leaping to her feet. "It's all very simple. I'll post some instructions through the door with the key in the morning."

"Hang on," said Mum. "You haven't said how long you'll be away for. Molly starts school on Monday."

"Just a couple of days. And I almost forgot," she said, turning to Molly, "while you're there could you feed Saffron's goldfish and Dylan's guinea pigs, and my husband's parrot, too? You're an angel! Right, I really must be off – we've got an early start."

She swept out of the room, leaving Molly's parents staring after her.

"Wow!" said Molly. "How exciting is that?"

"Indeed," said Dad. "Now please can I have my chips back?"

Chapter Five

The Beastie

Clatter went the letterbox. Then something landed on the doormat with a THUD.

Molly leaped out of bed and dashed downstairs in her pyjamas. There was a large, pink envelope on the doormat with her name on it. Molly tore it open, and a heavy gold key fell to the floor. She picked it up and peeped inside the

34

envelope. She pulled out a small sheet
of pink paper, and started to read...

Instructions.
1. Feed my daarling Mimi
2. Feed the Guinea Pigs
3. Feed Clive's Parrot
4. Polish the silverware
5. Mop the floors
6. Wash the windows
7. Water the plants.
8. Mow the lawn
9.
10.

Molly tucked the instructions into her
pyjama pocket, and ran up to her room
to get dressed. She was too excited to eat
breakfast. "Bye, Mum! Bye, Dad!" she
called to her sleeping parents. Then she
headed next door.

Molly skipped through the golden gates, around the fountain and up to the palace. She took the key from her pocket and unlocked the door. It swung open with a loud creak. There in front of her was a beautiful marble hallway, with a twisting staircase and a huge, glittering chandelier. Molly tiptoed inside.

"WOW," she said out loud, gazing around the room.

"Hello, my dear," said a high, wispy voice.

Molly froze. Who was that? Surely the Von Volavons were on holiday.

"Who's there?" called Molly, sounding braver than she felt.

A terrifying shadow appeared at the far end of the room. Molly's heart pounded. It must be the Beastie!

She was about to turn and run, when a small, perfectly round and spotlessly white Persian cat padded forwards. Molly couldn't believe her eyes. The cat was wearing clothes. It was dressed in a shocking-pink tutu, a tiara and tiny ballet shoes. Amazed, Molly watched as it pitter-pattered across the room and settled itself on a satin cushion.

Molly and the ballerina cat stared at each other for a second, then Molly started to giggle, and once she started she couldn't stop. She collapsed helplessly in a heap on the floor.

It was the most ridiculous thing she had ever seen!

The cat was not amused. "Just WHAT is so funny?" she hissed.

Molly's eyes widened. "Wow, a talking cat. How cool is that!"

"Cat?" said the cat. "I am no CAT. I am Madam Mimi Mew Mew Von Volavon the Third!" she said regally. "But you may call me Mimi."

"Pleased to meet you, Mimi," blurted Molly, doing a little curtsey. "My name's Molly. Are you ready for some breakfast, puss?" she asked, as she strolled through into the kitchen.

Molly gazed around the room. She had never seen such a large kitchen. "Now where does Mrs Von Volavon keep the cat dish?" she said to herself.

"In the second from top cupboard on the left," Mimi answered, her tail swishing impatiently.

Molly opened the cupboard and peered in. There was no obvious cat dish, so she took out a willow-patterned china bowl and a silver spoon.

Mimi watched as Molly placed the bowl on the floor. "Not my favourite," she sniffed, "but I suppose it will do."

Molly stifled a giggle, and opened a tin of Moggy Meat. "Come on, Mimi, breakfast time!"

The cat glared at her, then at the disgusting gunk that was being spooned into the bowl, and a look of pure horror swept over her face. She fixed Molly with a piercing stare.

"And just what is that?" she hissed.

Molly took no notice. "Come on, puss. Less talking more eating!"

"How DARE you talk to me like that! Don't you know who I am?" Mimi yowled.

"Yes, you're Mimi, my next-door neighbours' cat," said Molly bluntly.

Mimi gasped. Her back arched and her fur stuck up on end.

"You insolent child! Why, I am Queen of All I Survey! The Royal Duchess of the Land, the Princess of the Realm and Ruler of ALL the World!"

"Right," said Molly, matter of factly.

"But even queens have to eat!"

"The Queen of All I Survey does not even LOOK at such revolting 'food'. SHE demands the finest cuisine fit for a queen. And she demands it

NOW!"

"But Mimi, you're a cat!" said Molly.
"And cats eat cat food!"

"I am NOT a cat," sniffed Mimi,
pointing her stubby pink nose in the air.

"Yes you are! You're a cat! A strange,
talking one, I admit, but still a cat."

"Well, if I were a cat, do you think

I would be
wearing this?"
Mimi said,
twirling her
tutu with
great pride
and pointing
her paws.
"Well,
you're no
normal cat, that's
for sure, but Mimi,
you are a MOGGY!"

44

"ENOUGH! Off with her head!"
screeched Mimi to no one in particular.

Nothing happened.

There was an awkward pause. Mimi
gave her paw a little lick. Then, suddenly
remembering where she was and what
she'd been talking about, she shouted,
"I will never be a MOGGY! And I will
never ever eat that Moggy Meat!"

She flounced across the room and
scrabbled in her cat litter tray
– in a suspiciously
catlike fashion.

Molly looked at the can of Moggy Meat. "But this is what I've been asked to feed you. Isn't this what you normally have, Mimi?"

Mimi didn't reply. "I DEMAND..." she said, squatting very regally, her head peeking over the side of the plastic litter tray "...the finest Trout à la Maison." She pointed to Saffron's goldfish, who was swimming around in its bowl on top of the kitchen counter.

"I want it stuffed with red meow-meow berries, not blue ones – RED. I want it soaked in a prawn sauce, on a platter of fresh catty-kin catnip. Not dried, FRESH!" she stated splendidly, stepping out of her litter tray.

Molly stared at the ridiculous cat. "OK, Mimi, you win. One Trout à la Maison coming up!"

"Well, what are you waiting for?" said Mimi, trotting across the kitchen.

Molly looked down at the helpless goldfish. "Don't worry, little fish," she whispered. "I won't let her eat you!"

gulp

Chapter Six

Trout à la Molly

Mimi was a cat who wasted no time.
In the blink of an eye, she was wearing
a chef's hat and apron over her ballerina
costume.

"GET THE TROUT!" Mimi ordered,
pointing a paw at the goldfish.

"Mimi, wait! Surely the Queen of All
You Survey should have a starter?" said
Molly, with a cunning smile.

Mimi thought for a moment. "Yes, you're right!" she exclaimed. "The Queen of All I Survey must have a starter. And the finest dish fit for a queen! It would be rude not to," she said, swishing her beautiful, fluffy tail.

"And surely a queen should be waited on hand and foot," added Molly quickly, trying to think of a way to get the cat out of the kitchen. "Let me be the chef. I insist, Mimi. You are a queen, after all! Why don't you go and wait on your throne?"

"Yes, one shall have a starter and one shall wait on one's throne," said Mimi.

As she trotted out of the kitchen, she glared up at the goldfish.

"You're mine," Mimi whispered, licking her lips. "I can't wait to eat you." Then she flounced into the living room and settled on her pink velvet cushion.

Back in the kitchen, Molly spooned the gloopy Moggy Meat into the bowl.
It didn't look very yummy, she had to admit. She gazed around the vast room. *There must be something I can use*, she mused. Finally, her eye fell on a parsley plant on the window sill.

"That'll have to do." She yanked a few leaves off the plant and arranged them neatly around the bowl. She didn't hear

Mimi pitter-patter back into the kitchen.

Mimi was not a patient cat when it
came to food. Bored of waiting, she
leaped up on to the counter with an
effortless hop, and sidled over to the
goldfish bowl.

The poor goldfish was now swimming
around very nervously indeed.

Mimi licked her lips
and smiled. She
extended her claws
and dipped her fluffy,
white paw into
the bowl.

Mimi jumped back in shock. She had
never, ever been wet before, and
it was the strangest
feeling. She stared at
her soaking paw, with
a look of horror.

Molly picked up the
bowl of Moggy Meat, and
went to place it on the
floor. "Mimi, here's your starter, Your
Majes—" She caught sight of Mimi on the
kitchen counter and froze. "Oh no,
Saffron's goldfish!" she cried.

Molly looked from Mimi to the
goldfish bowl, and sighed with relief as
the fish swam cautiously out from behind
a piece of seaweed.

"REAOOOOOW!" meowed Mimi,
holding her bedraggled paw limply in the
air. "Look at the ROYAL PAW! Call the

doctor! I think I must be dying!" she
howled.

Molly took no notice. She didn't feel
sorry for Mimi one little bit. "Stop being
so ridiculous," she said, firmly. "It serves
you right for trying to—"

"OH, it's SO WET and SO COLD!"
interrupted Mimi. "AND ... it doesn't go
with my OUTFIT!" she howled. She
glared at Molly. "WELL DO
SOMETHING!"

Molly was trying hard not to laugh. "Poor puss, it'll dry…"

"Puss! I am no PUSS!" spat Mimi. She hobbled out of the room on her three dry legs and settled herself on her cushion.

It was time to go. Molly put the goldfish bowl on the highest shelf she could find. Then she refilled Mimi's water bowl and placed it on the floor next to the starter of Moggy Meat. *Hopefully Mimi will eat when she gets hungry*, she thought.

"Bye, Mimi. See you later!"

Chapter Seven

Pork de la Bon-Von-de-Mon

"So," said Mum as she handed Molly a cup of hot blackcurrant and a biscuit. "How was cat-sitting?"

Molly desperately wanted to tell her mum about the talking cat, but she knew it was just too impossible-to-believe. She could still hardly believe it herself!

"It was OK. A bit boring, actually," she muttered casually.

"Well, don't forget you've still got to go back over there this evening," said Mum. "We can't have that little puss starve. What would Mrs Von Volavon say?"

Molly smiled to herself. *More importantly, what would Mimi say?*

That evening, Molly skipped next door.

"Mimi! It's me, Molly, and guess what ... it's dinnertime!" she shouted. Her voice echoed down the glimmering hallway. There was no sign of Mimi.

In the kitchen, the cat's breakfast sat untouched on the floor. *Rats!* thought Molly.

Suddenly, there came the padding of fluffy feet. Molly spun round and came face to face with ... Little Bo Peep!

Mimi was wearing a blue bonnet lined

with delicate white frills, and a delightful
baby-blue apron. On her paws she wore
four frilly blue socks, and in her left
forepaw she carried a long crook with
a curly bit at the top.

Mimi trotted across the floor, sat down and innocently licked her paw.

Molly bit her lip and tried hard not to giggle.

"Um … Mimi, you seem to have lost your sheep!" she stammered, before exploding into a fit of laughter.

From under her blue bonnet, Mimi gave Molly a hard stare.

"Please excuse me, Your Highness," said Molly. "That was very rude of me. Now, are you ready for dinner?"

"I'm not eating any of your Moggy Muck!" Mimi declared.

"Oh, Mimi," Molly sighed. She gazed out of the window and caught sight of the guinea pig hutch.

"Well, if you're not going to eat, I'd better go and feed Dylan's guinea pigs," she said, cheerfully. "I'm sure they'll be pleased to see me!"

Ignoring Mimi, she took a handful of lettuce leaves from the fridge and headed out into the garden.

Molly watched as the two guinea pigs – Moo Moo and Dinky – eagerly tucked into their food.

"Are you enjoying that?" she said, almost expecting them to answer.

"Ah-hem!" From behind her, Molly heard the sound of someone clearing their throat. She turned round. It was Mimi – and she was looking crosser than ever.

"What about *my* dinner?"

"I haven't forgotten about you, Mimi," said Molly, politely. "Why, in the kitchen there's a delicious bowl of—"

But Mimi was in no mood to listen. "I DEMAND Roasted Pork de la Bon-Von-de-Mon in a truffle sauce," she said.

Molly gave her a puzzled look. "Pork de la Bon-Von-de-Mon," she repeated.

"Yes, now get the PORK!" snapped Mimi, pointing her curled crook in the direction of Dylan's guinea pigs.

"And make sure they are wearing their BONNETS!" Mimi added. At that moment, her own bonnet flopped down over her nose. "It adds to the flavour," she explained in a muffled voice.

"Mimi, you are quite ridiculous!" Molly laughed. "But if that's what you want, very well then. This evening the Lady of the Litter Tray shall dine on Roasted Pork de la Bon-Von-de-Mon!" Molly felt hopeful – she'd pretend to do just as Mimi ordered, if *that* was what it took to get her to eat.

Contented, Mimi flopped on to her back, and rolled over in a pile of leaves, her paws in the air.

At last! she thought. *I'm getting a dinner fit for a queen!*

Moo Moo and Dinky sat in their hutch, quietly nibbling on their lettuce leaves. Ever so slowly, Molly opened the door, and even slower still, she bent down.

"Here Dinky, here Moo Moo," she called loudly, making a half-hearted effort to scoop them up. As she did so, she spied Mimi out of the corner of her eye.

The cat had already lost interest. Molly watched as she stalked impatiently back to the house and disappeared through the cat flap.

Molly smiled to herself. So far things were going just as planned.

"Don't worry, my little friends," she said, closing the hutch door. "I'm not really going to cook you."

All she had to do now was convince Mimi that the meal she was about to eat was not Moggy Meat – it was pork of the finest quality, with a truffle sauce!

Chapter Eight

Pineapple Head

"Oh, Little Bo Peeee-eep!" sang Molly, walking slowly into the living room, carrying a silver dish. She carefully placed it on the coffee table and raised the lid to reveal two skilfully-moulded mounds of Moggy Meat, about guinea pig size, covered in a thin layer of gravy and topped with a sprig of dandelion from the lawn.

"Dinner is served," announced Molly.

"Meowww!" said Mimi, licking her lips. "I mean GOOOD!"

All of a sudden, Mimi froze. "Acck! *Acck!* Acck!" she coughed dramatically. Then "Acck! Acck! Acck!" again.

Molly was just about to come to Mimi's rescue, when the cat bent forward and out shot a white ball of fur.

Mimi glanced around, as if nothing had happened.

Just a fur ball. Phew! thought Molly. But then she remembered Mrs Von Volavon's list of instructions. *Oh no! Aren't I supposed to brush Mimi's fur once a day...?*

"Now, Mimi," said Molly in a calm, determined voice. "The Queen should look fit for her feast, don't you think?"

Mimi tilted her head to one side and stared up at Molly.

"Why don't you come through to the kitchen, and I'll give you a little groom," Molly said sweetly. "There's nothing better than a good brush before dinner," she added.

The cat's face said it all. She narrowed her blue eyes with a "nobody brushes me" sort of look.

Molly wasn't going to let this stop her. She bent down, and made a grab for Mimi.

But Mimi was surprisingly fast on her feet... "No, you don't!" she yowled, scuttling off across the room.

"In that case, I'll just have to chase you," declared Molly, and set off after her.

Round and round scampered Mimi, with Molly in hot purr-suit. Faster and faster they ran... Dizzier and dizzier became Mimi. Giddier and giddier became Molly.

But the chase went on...

Suddenly, without warning, Mimi came to a stop. One moment she was speeding round the table; the next she had paused to give herself a little wash. Molly, who was right behind, tumbled straight over her and skidded along the polished marble floor, her arms flailing wildly. "Whooooa!"

She reached out for the sideboard to stop herself ... and knocked over a large vase of pink tulips.

Water and tulips flew everywhere. Mimi leaped out of the way, but she wasn't quite quick enough...

Molly looked up to see Mimi sat in a puddle of water.

"LOOK AT MY BEAUTIFUL TAIL!" yowled Mimi. She stood up and stalked over to Molly, her tail drooping behind her, leaving a trail of water.

Mimi's eyes narrowed with rage...

"PINEAPPLE HEAD!"
she screeched at Molly.

"My OUTFIT is RUINED and my tail is all wet. And it's YOUR fault," she growled furiously. She stomped over to her velvet cushion and there she sat in a big, black mood.

Molly could feel Mimi's sulky gaze as she mopped up the pool of water and attempted to straighten out the tulips. Then a quick sweep here and another little mop there, and the room looked almost as good as new.

But the dish of cleverly-disguised Moggy Meat still lay untouched on the table. Molly picked it up and looked over at Mimi with a pleading smile.

"Don't even think about it," hissed Mimi. "I've lost my appetite!"

"Very well, Mimi," replied Molly.

"But I'll leave it here just in case you feel hungry later on. I'll see you tomorrow," she said, giving the cross cat a wave goodbye.

"And tomorrow I'm just going to have to try even harder," she said to herself under her breath.

Chapter Nine

Mimi Meets a Talking Quail

Molly was quieter than usual the next morning over breakfast. She munched thoughtfully on her toast. *There must be some way of getting Mimi to eat... What I need is a plan...*

Dad helped himself to another slice. "So, Molly, tell us about cat-sitting."

"Oh, Dad," said Molly. She rolled her eyes theatrically, stretched out her arms and gave a big YAWN. "You really don't want to know. It's really dull, honestly."

After breakfast, Molly walked up the drive to Palace Von Volavon with a cookbook under her arm. As far as plans went it wasn't a very good one, but it would have to do.

Maybe, just maybe, Mimi has got hungry enough to eat her Moggy Meat, she thought hopefully. But from what she knew of Mimi, it wasn't very likely. Molly shuddered as she remembered her mum's words – she couldn't let the poor cat starve, however badly Mimi had behaved.

"Good morning, Mimi!" chirped Molly in her most cheerful voice, as she flung open the door. "It's a lovely day, and it's breakfast time!"

Silence.

Molly headed straight for the living room and peered in. As predicted, the dish of Moggy Meat lay untouched on the table. Molly glanced over at the velvet cushion – no Mimi.

Molly wandered into the kitchen, placed the cookbook on the counter and tipped the dish of food into the bin.

Still no Mimi. So where was the little Madam?

Just then, she heard the faint sound of voices coming from a room at the end of the hallway. *Are the Von Volavons back already?* worried Molly. *Surely not!*

She hurried down the hall, pushed open the door, and was confronted by piles and piles of papers. The room was lined with numerous dusty books, maps and globes. It was Mr Von Volavon's study.

"Scaredy-cat!"

came a rasping cry from the corner.

"HOW DARE YOU!" said a very offended voice. Although Molly couldn't see her, she knew it was Mimi.

"Scaredy-cat! Scaredy-cat! Scaredy-cat!" chanted the other voice.

"I've had enough of you!" hissed Mimi.

Who was Mimi talking to? Molly wondered. She crept quietly round the desk, careful not to disturb any of the piles of paper.

In the corner sat Mimi. Today she was dressed as a Red Indian, complete with feathered headdress, breastplate and a quiver of arrows tied to her back. In her paw was a small bow.

She was looking intently up at the ceiling. Molly followed her gaze. There hung an ornate gold cage, with a plump red and blue bird inside. Mr Von Volavon's parrot.

"AAAAWWWK!" squawked the parrot.

"How DARE you speak to me like that!" gasped Mimi. "Don't you know who I am?"

Molly ducked behind a bookshelf to watch.

"Scaredy-cat! Scaredy-cat! Scaredy-cat!" retorted the parrot.

"I most certainly am not!" cried Mimi. "I am Pokka-chonkus the Brave, and I am NOT scared, and I am MOST CERTAINLY NOT A CAT!"

Molly giggled quietly from her hiding place. "AAAAWWWK!" squawked the parrot again.

Mimi narrowed her eyes dangerously. "RIGHT, THAT'S IT!" she hissed, drawing an arrow and aiming it at the bird.

"Mimi, NOOOOOO!" shouted Molly.

Pokka-chonkus the Brave swivelled round to glare at Molly. Then she completely forgot what she was doing, dropped the bow and, in true cat-fashion, pounced at a ball of paper on the floor beside the bin.

"What were you doing, Mimi?" said Molly, horrified.

"Oh, it's you!" said Mimi. "I've got to say I thought *you* were dull. But at least you're better company than that

imbecile up there." She waved a paw in the direction of the cage. "He's got a very limited vocabulary."

"Don't change the subject," said Molly. "What were you doing just then?"

"Nothing whatsoever..." said the cat in her most innocent voice.

"In that case, Mimi, follow me. It's breakfast time," said Molly firmly.

Mimi straightened her headdress and trotted after Molly obediently, then stopped as a glimmer of memory from yesterday flashed through her head.

"Wait a moment," said Mimi. "You're not going to try and feed me that Moggy Muck again!" she cried, scampering back towards the study.

"Oh no you don't, puss!" said Molly, grabbing the quiver of arrows tied to the cat's back. Enough was enough.

"YOU'RE A CAT! AND CATS EAT CAT FOOD!" cried Molly.

"Never!" screamed Mimi, wriggling free. "I DEMAND Roasted Talking Quail," she declared, pointing at the parrot.

"I want that quail on a purr-fect bed of mewkin-meow-mew sauce, sprinkled with mew-sli, obviously," she added. She licked her lips. "NOW GET MY TALKING QUAIL!"

Chapter
Ten

Pokka-chonkus the Brave Stalks a Quail

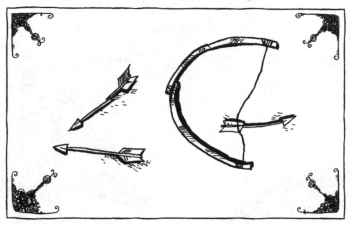

Now, even for Molly, this situation was getting out of control. She had to find a way of getting Mimi to eat – something other than the parrot, that was – and fast.

But first, she needed a cunning way to distract Mimi while she prepared the Moggy Meat.

Suddenly, inspiration struck.

"You know, Mimi, Talking Quail is one of my favourite dishes, too," she said. "So I hope you don't mind if I join you." Then Molly frowned. "But we only have one quail," she said with a sigh.

"Mimi … um, I mean Pokka-chonkus the Brave … do you think you could help me catch another quail…?"

Mimi looked interested at this, so Molly continued.

"…You'll have to hunt it, with bows and arrows," said Molly. "Do you think you could do that?"

Mimi's ears pricked up. "Why, I have a bow and arrow! It's purr-fect!" she purred. "I will hunt!"

"You know I think I saw lots of quails, in the, the ... that way!" said Molly, pointing in the opposite direction to the kitchen.

Mimi drew her bow and arrow and charged off.

Molly clapped her hands and hurried into the kitchen. She had to get the Moggy Meat ready and hide the parrot before Mimi worked out there were no quails.

Molly quickly spooned the gloopy Moggy Meat into a dish, and moulded it with a fork into the shape of a quail. Then she dashed back into the study.

"Scaredy-cat, scaredy-cat," retorted the parrot, as Molly entered. "Scaredy—"

Molly threw a heavy velvet cloth over the cage, silencing the parrot.

Meanwhile, Mimi prowled around the living room, her bow and arrow at the ready. She had some serious quail catching to do.

Suddenly she froze in horror. "What if the girl has tricked me?" she said out loud. "What if she wants to eat the talking quail herself?"

Mimi raced back into the study and leaped up on to the desk. "Yooowl!" howled Mimi. The parrot and its cage had disappeared.

There was no time to waste. But as Mimi leaped to the floor, she brushed against a towering pile of paper, which swayed dangerously. On top of this, an ancient half-full mug of hot chocolate wobbled, then plummeted to the ground. Mimi glanced up and saw the cup hurtling towards her. She tried to dart out of the way, but it was too late.

SPLASH!

went the cup of hot chocolate as it
landed right on Mimi's head, staining her
white front a dark, muddy brown.
Papers and blueprints fluttered down
around her, and stuck to her chocolate-
coated fur.

In the kitchen, Molly was putting the finishing touches to breakfast. "Mimi, food time!" she called.

Molly looked up as Mimi trailed miserably into the room. "Oh, Mimi, what have you done now!" she cried. She burst out laughing at the chocolatey, paper-covered cat.

"Serves you right, Mimi Von Volavon," said Molly. "Now will you eat your Moggy Meat ... I mean, Roasted Talking Quail?"

"Never!" said Mimi. Then she started to furiously lick her matted fur.

Chapter Eleven

Swan Lake

Back at Molly's home, it was a normal Sunday afternoon. Mum was repotting a plant and Dad was reading the newspaper. *Boring*, thought Molly.

She settled down on the sofa and flicked throught the TV channels. There were only the usual dreary Sunday programmes about gardening and the countryside.

The countryside... Yes, life in Fuffleton would be a bit dull without Mimi, Molly said to herself. Then she had a horrible thought. Tomorrow the Von Volavons would be back, and that would be the end of her trips to see Mimi.

Molly leaped up. She'd spend the rest of the day with the cat. *And I won't even try to get her to eat any Moggy Meat,* she decided. *Not if she doesn't want to.* After all, she almost felt sorry for the little fluffball.

Molly skipped up the Von Volavons'
driveway, and skirted round the fountain.
In the water sat a beautifully white and
pristine swan.

Molly swung open the front door.
"Oh, Mimi!" she called. "Are you there?"
This time Molly had no trouble finding
Mimi – there was a very
obvious trail of clues
leading to the cat, who
was sitting at the
bottom of the stairs.

There was something different about Mimi this afternoon. Dark-brown stains covered her matted fur, which was dotted with sheets of paper.

To Molly's surprise, Mimi wasn't wearing an outfit, only her little tiara, which sat crookedly on her head.

"Mimi, is anything the mat—" Molly began.

"Swan," said Mimi under her breath.

"Swan?" replied Molly, confused.

"I DEMAND…"

"Oh, here we go!" said Molly.

"…the largest roasted SWAN in the world, stuffed with the freshest catty-kin catnip, marinated in red ooger-Balouga sauce.

I want it NOW

and I want it HERE

and I want it wearing its tutu and socks!" she stated splendidly.

"With a little salt and vinegar to season," she added quietly.

Molly was not in the mood. She had set out to be nice to Mimi, but the cat was being just as difficult and ungrateful as usual.

"I will do no such thing, Mimi, this is ridiculous!" said Molly.

"WHAAAT?"

"How many times do I have to tell you?" shouted Molly. "You are a moggy, a CAT! A crazy moggy, but still a cat."

"I AM NOT, AND I WILL NEVER BE A COMMON MOGGY!" Mimi screamed, her tail fluffing up with anger.

"I am a pure-bred Persian, in case you don't know. And I WANT MY ROASTED SWAN, AND I WANT IT NOW!" She pointed at the open door with a bedraggled, brown paw.

Molly looked outside at the swan on the fountain. "No, I'm not doing it," she said, folding her arms.

"Well, I'll get it MYSELF!" shrieked Mimi. "To the FOUNTAIN!" she declared, as if rallying an army.

"MIMI, NO!" shouted Molly. She blocked the doorway. But Mimi slipped through her legs and bolted down the drive towards the swan.

She leaped delicately on to the edge of the fountain and picked up a net for clearing out leaves that was lying on the grass nearby.

Mimi was already teetering on the edge of the fountain, when Molly caught her up. She was waving the net in the air, and hissing at the swan.

The swan paid Mimi no attention whatsoever. She bent her long, white neck and gracefully preened her gleaming white feathers.

"Beautiful," sighed Molly.

Mimi frowned. "Nobody is more beautiful than ME!" declared the cat, prancing along the edge of the fountain.

The swan fluttered her wings, and waggled her tail feathers. Mimi scowled. She looked down at her reflection in the water and saw her chocolate-covered fur sticking up on end, her tiara tilting to one side. Her blue eyes flashed with envy. She let out an almightly howl,

"That swan must DIE..."

Chapter Twelve

Soggy Moggy

Strange things happen inside the brain of
a cat – particularly a pure-bred Persian –
when it goes without food for a day or
two and when it gets slightly
wet, mucky and sticky.
Indeed, when that
situation occurs, there is
no telling what might
happen...

"I can't reach the swan from here. Help me, you peasant!" shouted Mimi to Molly at the top of her voice. Molly watched as Mimi sprang on to the bronze fish at the centre of the fountain, and began to climb up it, with the net between her teeth.

The swan glanced at the cat, then flapped her white wings. She waggled her tail, and glided across the water as if she was in a glitzy fashion show.

"I AM THE FAIREST IN THE LAND!" yelled Mimi. She scrabbled to the top of the fish. Gathering all the grace she could muster, she stood on two legs and twirled around and around. Suddenly, there was a rumble, a clicking sound, and then...

WHOOOOSH!

Water gushed from the mouth of the fish, shooting the pirouetting cat into the air. Then, as quickly as it had started, the jet of water was gone. And so was Mimi.

Molly gasped. "Oh no, what will Mrs Von Volavon say? I am in deep trouble," she panicked.

From the flower bed behind the fountain there was a faint meowing. Molly ran in the direction of the noise. There, wedged in a rose bush, was a very sorry sight. Matted and dripping, her tail drooping, was Mimi – never in her life had she been quite so soggy. Molly rushed over and dragged the bedraggled cat from out of the bush.

"Mimi, are you OK?"

"BLUB,"

blubbed Mimi, blowing a bubble from her nose.

The cat sat up. She appeared sort of ... woozy. She pointed a sodden paw into the air, took a deep breath and said, " I DEMAN—" Then fainted.

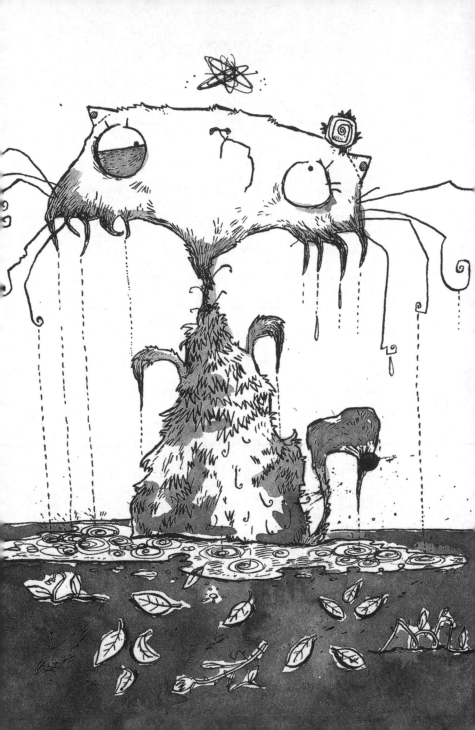

Mimi awoke on her velvet cushion. She opened her eyes to see Molly's concerned face gazing down at her. Mimi gave a quiet, pitiful, "Reeoow!"

"Mimi, it's not so bad…" said Molly, kindly. And it wasn't. At least the water from the fountain had cleaned the hot chocolate from her fur. And a pink rose had got caught behind her ear. She actually looked rather pretty.

"Mimi," said Molly gently. "I thought you might be hungry. But you don't have to eat anything if you don't want to."

Mimi glanced over at the
bowl of brown gloop sitting
there in front of her. Then
she dared to have a little sniff.

Sniff, sniff, sniff...

Her stomach grumbled.
To Mimi's great surprise, it
actually smelled delicious.

Mimi hadn't eaten all
weekend and, if truth be told,
she was STARVING! As her tummy
grumbled again, she leaned over
her bowl and took a small bite.

Inside the cat's mouth, her taste
buds flurried and whizzed, popped
and fizzled.

Suddenly she sat bolt upright.
Her eyes widened.

Molly held her breath
in suspense...

"Yes, I would say a flurry of flavours...
A little roasted pork definitely from the
Bon-Von-de-Mon region, a hint of trout,
definitely à la Maison, the truffle sauce
is just sublime and I can honestly say the
pork was, on this occasion, definitely
wearing its bonnet!" purred Mimi.

"Now, I DEMAND..." she declared.

Molly sighed.

"...another bowlful, please. Because
this is DELICIOUS!"

Molly breathed a huge sigh of relief,
as Mimi licked her dish clean.

What a weekend! thought Molly. *And I thought my new life in the countryside was going to be boring. But I'VE NEVER HAD SO MUCH FUN! Still, look at all this mess.*

Mimi watched as Molly gathered up empty tins of Moggy Meat, soggy garments, a crook with a curly handle and a fishing net, and swept them under a large, luxurious rug.

"Nobody will ever know. Right, Soggy Moggy!" she winked at Mimi.

A look of absolute horror and offence swept across the cat's face... Then a look of confusion, then...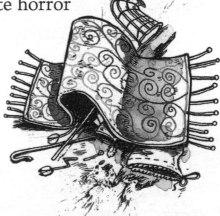

"ZZZZZ..." Well fed and exhausted, Mimi had completely forgotten what Molly had just called her, and was now having a long overdue catnap on the sofa. She purred loudly and Molly gave her a gentle stroke.

I wish I could come back tomorrow, she thought. *But the Von Volavons will be home, and anyway I'm starting my new school.*

As she tiptoed towards the door, the sound of loud, happy purring echoed around the palace.

I've become quite fond of that little fluffball, reflected Molly.

She gave Mimi one last look, and smiled like a Cheshire cat.

"Hope to see you again soon, Mimi!"

A real flurry

Glorious chunks of pork from the Bon-Von-de-Mon region and a hint of Trout à la Maison, in a simply sublime truffle sauce.

And look out for Molly and Mimi's
next purr-fect adventure